First published in the United States, Great Britain, Canada,
Australia and New Zealand in 1990 by North-South Books,
an imprint of Rada Matija AG,
8625 Gossau ZH, Switzerland.

Library of Congress Catalog Card Number: 89-43249
Library of Congress Cataloging in Publication Data is available.
ISBN 1-55858-084-0
Moers, Hermann, *1930-*
Tonio the great.
I. Title II. Wilkoń, Józef
III. Tonio auf dem Hochseil. *English*
833'.914 [J]

ISBN 1-55858-084-0

1   3   5   7   9   10   8   6   4   2
Printed in Germany

TONIO THE GREAT

By Hermann Moers
Illustrated by Józef Wilkoń

North-South Books / New York

Tonio the Great was the finest acrobat in the circus. He could do backflips and handstands, somersaults and flying leaps. He could hang from a trapeze, held on by his toes, and he could balance a chair on the tip of his nose.

But he was called Tonio the Great because of the dangerous feats he could perform on the tightrope, high above the audience.

Dressed in beautiful costumes, Tonio and his wife Pamela would climb up the rope-ladder while the orchestra played a drum roll. Tonio would jump on his unicycle and Pamela would balance herself upside down on his head. Everyone down below would stop breathing for a moment as they watched the fearless couple ride slowly across the thin tightrope to the other side.

One day, while Tonio was performing
with the other acrobats, he saw a sparrow
flying above his head. The sparrow was
so interested in everything happening
inside the tent, that he flew into a pole
and fell to the ground.

Tonio climbed down as quickly as he could and gently picked up the poor sparrow. The bird was alive and soon he was ready to fly away. But before the sparrow left, Tonio was certain that he heard the tiny bird say, "Be careful, Tonio, or you'll end up falling — just like me!"

The very next night, when he climbed up the rope-ladder, Tonio looked down at the audience far below. He suddenly remembered the way the little bird had fluttered to the ground. His knees trembled and sweat began to drip down his face. For the first time in his life, Tonio the Great was afraid.

As he clung to the rope-ladder, Tonio could hear the audience talking about him. "What's wrong?" someone asked. "I thought this guy was supposed to be the greatest." "I want my money back!" yelled someone else.

When the ringmaster saw Tonio start to climb back down the ladder, he announced that Tonio was sick and would be unable to perform. Everyone in the audience was upset.

"What am I going to do?" said Tonio. "No one wants to see an acrobat who's too scared to perform."

Tonio went to the animal tamer to ask him for advice. He looks so brave, thought Tonio, as he watched the animal tamer perform his act. He makes wild animals jump through burning hoops and even puts his head in a lion's mouth!

Tonio asked the animal tamer how he could do such dangerous things without being scared. The animal tamer thought for a moment and said, "You don't understand, Tonio. I'm always scared when I get in this cage. But an animal tamer must never let the animals know that he is afraid."

The next day, during practice, Tonio tried to hide his fear. He climbed right to the top of the highest ladder in the circus tent. But just as he was about to swing out on a trapeze he became dizzy and had to climb right back down again.

Later, as Tonio sat on the steps of his trailer, Anton the Clown stopped to comfort him. "Cheer up, my friend," Anton said softly. "I think I know a way to help you."

The ringmaster was also upset. Since Tonio had stopped performing the audience had become smaller and smaller.

Anton put his big gloved hand on the ringmaster's shoulder. "Don't worry," he said with a smile. "Tonio and I think we've found a way for him to perform his act."

"Ladies and gentlemen," said the ringmaster at the beginning of the next performance. "It's my pleasure to introduce a new act: Stumbling Sam, the acrobatic clown!"

Everyone in the audience laughed. Stumbling Sam had a shiny bald head and huge shoes which made him waddle like a duck. What no one in the audience realized was that Stumbling Sam was really Tonio the Great in disguise.

True to his name, Stumbling Sam could barely climb up the ladder without falling halfway down again. There he was, clinging fearfully to the ladder as the audience laughed.

When he reached the tightrope he climbed onto a unicycle and started to ride across. But after a few feet he seemed to realize how dangerous the unicycle really was and rode furiously back to the platform.

While the audience was still laughing he stood up proudly, pulled his little cap over his bald head and shot out to the middle of the tightrope. Next, he spun around and cycled the rest of the way across — *backwards*.

The audience gasped. Only Tonio the Great had been able to perform such a dangerous feat.

Soon Pamela climbed up the rope-ladder. She too, was dressed as a clown.

The audience laughed as she pretended to push Stumbling Sam back out on the tightrope. But even though he looked frightened, Stumbling Sam performed the most amazing acrobatic tricks anyone had ever seen.

The audience jumped up and clapped when Stumbling Sam finished his performance. The ringmaster waved his baton, Pamela blew him a kiss, and Anton the Clown gave him the thumbs-up sign. Many people said that Stumbling Sam was a better act than Tonio the Great. He could do all the great feats, like Tonio, but he was also very funny.

As he stood in the circle before the crowd, listening to what they said, Tonio the Great just smiled.

LL   Moers, Hermann
P   Tonio The Great
MOE

08/2011	DATE DUE		